D1609435

Molly the Great Respects the Flag:

A Book About Being a Good Citizen

by Shelley Marshall   Illustrated by Ben Mahan

Being a good citizen is when you pitch in. You help make the world a better place. **Let's read!**

Hi! I'm Molly!

Enslow Elementary
an imprint of
Enslow Publishers, Inc.
40 Industrial Road
Box 398
Berkeley Heights, NJ 07922
USA

http://www.enslow.com

"Hello, Rabbit Rangers!" says Mrs. Nibbler. "Next week is the Fourth of July parade. And, guess what?"

"Our troop gets to carry the flag!"

3

"I need one girl to hold the flag. The rest of us will march behind her."

"Candy, would you carry the flag?"

5

At home, Molly throws her vest on the floor.

"I'm not going to the parade!" she yells.

"What's wrong?" Molly's mom asks.

"I want to carry the flag!" Molly cries.

6

7

"But you are part of the troop. You have to go to the parade."

"OK," says Molly. "But I will not smile."

9

It is time for the parade. What is Candy doing?

"I'm putting stickers on the flag," says Candy.

"Wait!" says Molly. "There are rules for carrying the flag! Never put stickers or anything else on the flag."

"Thanks, Molly," says Candy. "You are a flag hero!"

13

"The flag is so big," says Candy. "It's hard to hold."

15

16

"Wait!" says Molly. "Never carry the flag upside down."

"Thanks, Molly. You are a flag hero!"

18

"The flag is too heavy," says Candy. "My arms are tired."

"Wait!" yells Molly. "The flag must never touch the ground."

"I have an idea," says Candy. "We can carry the flag together."

"Now we are both flag heroes!"

Read More About Being a Good Citizen

Books

Kroll, Virginia. *Good Citizen Sarah*. Morton Grove, IL: Albert Whitman & Company, 2007.

Mayer, Cassie. *Being Helpful*. Chicago: Heinemann Library, 2008.

Web Site

Kids Next Door

www.hud.gov/kids/people.html

Enslow Elementary, an imprint of Enslow Publishers, Inc.

Enslow Elementary® is a registered trademark of Enslow Publishers, Inc.

Copyright © 2010 by Enslow Publishers, Inc.

Library of Congress Cataloging-in-Publication Data
Marshall, Shelley, 1968-
  Molly the Great respects the flag : a book about being a good citizen / Shelley Marshall.
    p. cm.
  ISBN 978-0-7660-3519-5
  1. Citizenship—Juvenile literature. I. Title.
  JF801.M357 2009
  323.6'50973—dc22

                    2009000497

ISBN-13: 978-0-7660-3744-1 (paperback edition)

Printed in the United States of America

112009 Lake Book Manufacturing, Inc., Melrose Park, IL

10 9 8 7 6 5 4 3 2 1

To Our Readers: We have done our best to make sure all Internet Addresses in this book were active and appropriate when we went to press. However, the author and the publisher have no control and assume no liability for the material available on those Internet sites or on other Web sites they may link to. Any comments or suggestions can be sent by e-mail to comments@enslow.com or to the address on the back cover.

♻ Enslow Publishers, Inc. is committed to printing our books on recycled paper. The paper in every book contains 10% to 30% post-consumer waste (PCW). The cover board on the outside of every book contains 100% PCW. Our goal is to do our part to help young people and the environment too!